Here She Lies

LIANA BROOKS

OTHER WORKS

ALL I WANT FOR CHRISTMAS

All I Want For Christmas Is A Reaper
All I Want For Christmas Is A Werewolf

FLEET OF MALIK

Bodies In Motion
Change of Momentum

HEROES AND VILLAINS

Even Villains Fall In Love
Even Villains Go To The Movies
Even Villains Have Interns
Even Villains Play The Hero (books 1 – 3 omnibus)
The Polar Terror

TIME AND SHADOWS

The Day Before
Convergence Point
Decoherence

SHORTER WORKS

Fey Lights
Prime Sensations
Darkness and Good

Find other works by the author at
www.lianabrooks.com

Here She Lies

INKLET #80

LIANA BROOKS

Inkprint PRESS

www.inkprintpress.com

Print ISBN: 978-1-922434-30-2
eBook ISBN: 9798201827625

www.inkprintpress.com

National Library of Australia Cataloguing-in-Publication Data
Brooks, Liana 1982 –
Here She Lies
54 p.
ISBN: 978-1-922434-30-2
Inkprint Press, Canberra, Australia
1. Fiction—Science Fiction—Action & Adventure 2. Fiction—Science Fiction—Crime & Mystery 3. Fiction—Romance—Science Fiction 4. Fiction—Short Stories

First Print Edition: April 2022
Cover photo © Diana Mironenko via Deposit Photos
Cover design © Inkprint Press
Interior art © Amy Laurens

HERE SHE LIES

Perhaps the dress was a little much. It was a yearly party to celebrate the company and most other people had come in the same clothes they'd worn last time. Some had even come straight from work.

Esana paused outside the main ballroom and looked at the gold-tinted mirror. The white dress had been bought years ago on a whim, shimmering white with a teardrop neckline that clasped around her neck and plummeted down in a slinky slide of snowy crystals with a generous scoop to display her cleavage. It had sat at the back of her closet all this time and it wasn't going to be too many more years before eating too much at her desk and forgetting to workout made the dress unwearable.

She twisted. If she looked better than everyone else at the party, so be it. That was the price they would have to pay for not putting in the effort.

A loud laugh broke out and then thunderous applause as the lights died and the main entertainment began. A concert with live performers. The room felt crowded even from the wrong side of the door.

Come this way, the stairs whispered. *Up on the balcony. Away from the crowds. You'll be safe here. No one will notice.*

It was a good idea. After all, she'd made an appearance, greeted everyone who needed to see her in attendance, and there was no one saving a seat on the main floor. On an empty balcony she could enjoy the concert and then escape as soon as everything was over.

The long dress pooled around her feet and made her take the stairs with a slow, regal step that would have made her co-workers laugh. Elegant and beautiful were not words they'd ever apply to her. She lifted her chin and pretended to be a princess, sweeping up the staircase... But to what?

A love? How dull.

A secret meeting? Too work-ish.

An intelligence conference? Yes, that would be where she was if she were a princess, taking intelligence reports and spinning those reports into actionable plans to save her people or expand the trade routes.

"Thank the stars for marketing." *There, but for the grace of quick thinking, go I.*

She reached the top of the stairs and relaxed a little, listening to the mur-

mur of voices. The boxes to the right were all full, but there were three to the left, close to the service elevator and the back stairs, that sounded like they were empty. Smiling, she turned to-ward them.

There was a crack of gunfire as the cymbals crashed inside the concert hall.

Esana froze, listening, but there were no screams. Maybe it had been her imagination. A drum beat that sounded too much like her neighborhood on a bad night.

When she was confident no one was screaming for help, she moved forward again.

The service door slammed open and Lev Sevastionovich stumbled through, glassy-eyed. He focused on her and sucked air through his teeth. "What are you doing here?"

"I... was coming to see if everyone had drinks," Esana lied.

He had his hand up under his shirt.

"Can I get you anything, Sevastionovich?" She used the politest term she could, not the indifferent Mr. Aleksiev or the too familiar Lev, but a name that recognized his place in the company. "Wine perhaps?"

"No. I'm fine."

He pushed away from the service door and all but fell through the door to the private balcony.

Esana hurried as fast as the skirt would allow. "Sir—"

He was waiting in the door frame. "Leave."

"I can—"

"Leave. I want to be alone." It hardly took an empathic skill to feel the injury radiating on his side or realize he was moments away from passing out. "As you say, sir." She bowed her head and turned away, an obedient drone.

The door closed behind her and she counted to ten, long enough for Sevastionovich to find his seat, and then she felt his mind crumble into darkness. He was going to die of blood loss on the balcony of a company party and the day would be forever marred.

Inexcusable.

Thankfully the company had been renting the hall for every major event since she'd joined six years ago, and in that time no one had ever moved the first-aid kit. She found it and checked the contents. Bandages, a patch to improve blood clotting times, a rehydration and antibiotic patch, and at the very bottom a pack of stimulant pills that could wake the dead. Not even expired.

But no cleansing wipes.

She'd need the wine after all.

Sweeping the train of her skirt into her hands she used the folds of the white gown to hide the med kit while she carried the wine in her other hand. She even rapped her knuckles on the door in case someone checked the cameras later. "Mister Aleksiev? Sevastionovich?" The door opened under slight pressure.

Music swelled around, a grand triumphant crescendo as the door snicked shut, locking her in the gloom of the private box.

She twitched the curtains back enough to give her a sliver of light and surveyed the patient.

Sevastionovich was passed out in the first seat, his shirt still in his hand. At least he'd managed to get that off before he collapsed. There was blood pooling on his dark pants, but that would probably go unnoticed.

Esana uncorked the wine, splashed it on a sanitary gauze and washed the wound. A simple graze. So the collapse was less likely to be from blood loss and more from shock. That happened sometimes. Being shot was never an easy thing.

As the orchestra played a running melody with angry horns blaring behind them, Esana cleaned the wound and applied the patches. She put the pills on Sevastionovich's tongue and tipped wine into his mouth. She checked his pulse.

It was only when she stood up again that she saw the smear of red blood across her torso. Nothing else had gone right all day, but at least she'd been right about the dress: she'd never be able to wear it again.

The door handle rattled.

Sevastionovich groaned, turning his head away from the sound.

Explaining this would require getting the boss involved. It would mean meetings, paperwork, and an unpleasant evening when her job depended on everything being pleasant. On the other hand, lying required only that she put her dignity on the line. It wasn't worth much anyway. She grabbed Sevastionivich's jacket and pulled it on, then pulled the pin from her hair and let it fall loose.

There was a knock at the door.

"Coming!" She giggled as she draped Sevastionovich's shirt over the bandages. "A moment, please!"

Putting on the smile she usually reserved for lucrative clients, she opened the door just enough to put one jacket-clad shoulder out and beam at the visitors.

Cecil stared at her.

"Cecil! How are you? I was..." Esana paused and looked back over her shoulder. "Um... diverted." She giggled again.

A bright flush of second-hand embarrassment and jealousy rushed through Cecil.

"Can I help you with something?" She batted her eyes at the two men in dark security suits standing behind him. "Is something wrong?"

"Ma'am," one of the men took off his cap, "we're with the portside security force. Have you seen anyone with a gunshot this evening?"

"A... a gunshot?" She widened her eyes in shock. "No. Why... Cecil, is everything perfectly all right?" She pushed the door wide, hugging the jacket over the bloodstain on her dress. "If anything ruins this party we will both be looking for work and I won't be giving you a good recommendation." The anger burned at the top of her mind, keeping out an intrusion from the men, although they didn't feel like empaths.

Cecil shook his head. "Nothing's wrong! I did nothing wrong."

"Someone was shot outside," the security officer said.

Esana raised her eyebrows in confused alarm. "Who?"

The security guards exchanged glances. They shared a mutual concern for privacy with a pressing need to find their victim. "There's a unregistered intelligence operative who came on planet this week," one said finally. "We were tracking them and successfully shot them, but didn't render them—"

"Dead?" Esana finished for him.

All three men were shocked.

"We weren't able to slow the intruder," the second guard said.

There was another exchange of glances.

"Ma'am, we need to inspect the box," the second security guard said.

Esana took a deep, heaving breath that made the crystals of her dress sparkle as her breasts rose and fell. "Um..." *Thank you acting classes where I learned to blush on command.* "...Could you perhaps, give us a moment? We're..." She laughed. "...I mean I'm not..."

She cleared her throat and looked at the ground in embarrassment.

Cecil turned bright red. "It's all well, Esana. Who—who are you here with?"

"Ah..." That was a little trickier.

If she could keep Cecil from knowing then tomorrow wouldn't be nearly as large as a disaster.

Of course, if the guards walked in and saw the blood, the troubles she'd have would include jail time. Esana started to close the door. It caught on something. She looked up at a strong, tanned hand, and the unbuttoned cuffs of an expensive white shirt.

"She is with me," Sevastionovich said.

Lev leaned against the doorframe to keep from pitching forward. The stimulants the girl had slipped him had gotten him moving, but his head was still swimming. He looked down. There was little to see but lush brown hair, his jacket hiding a beautifully sculpted body, and a white dress that should have looked tacky but was instead contributing to his inability to breathe properly.

As soon as the guards were gone, he'd have to figure out how this had happened.

"Sevastionovich!" Cecil looked up at him in shock. "Esana!"

So that was her name. It suited her.

"I can explain!" Esana said breathlessly, leaning forward just enough to rivet everyone's attention, burning away all the oxygen. "Um... Where do I start?" She looked up at him through long black lashes, eyes filled with admiration he knew she didn't feel.

"Start at the beginning, my charm. That summer we met."

She laughed happily. "Of course! Lev and I knew each other from the Port Royale Resort. I worked there over the summer and his family always vacationed there." She snuck him another appreciative glance. "He would be swimming when I came to change the flowers every afternoon. Even then he was handsome." Her eyes caressed him shamelessly.

The security guard pulled out a notebook. "Do you recall the address?"

"Mmm." Esana closed her eyes. "I forget the house number, but the door was yellow, and the house was blue, with a white roof. It was on Forsythe Lane along the western shore of the peninsula."

Lev stared. That was the family's summer house. He could remember the smell of honeysuckle on the evening tide.

"There was a smell of honeysuckle, and in the evening there was woodsmoke from the pizza grill." Her smile was a joyful indulgence, as if she were recalling her happiest memory.

"You said you didn't know him!" Cecil complained.

Esana dipped her eyes and her cheeks turned rosy. "I didn't really introduce myself properly. It wasn't a formal meeting. But, you know how it is in the summer time. You meet so many interesting people, and one thing led to another. I didn't think I'd see him again, but when we saw each other the other day there was..." She paused to look up at him again.

Lev looked down at her and raised an eyebrow.

"Chemistry," she said.

Antagonism would have been more accurate, but hate was a sort of chemistry too.

"An indescribable something. We wound up talking and reconnecting." She shrugged elegantly.

Cecil crossed his arms.

"You heard nothing?" the security officer asked.

"Oh, I heard plenty." Esana's tone was suggestive. "But with the orchestra and other sounds I'm afraid I didn't hear anything outside our little reunion. Did you, Lev?"

His smile this time was real. "I heard many things, my charm, but none of them were gunshots. Mostly moans." He drew the word out to feel her reaction, but there was nothing.

This Esana was cold as winter water under her sultry smiles. Unruffled by the guards or the blood.

Lev gathered his strength and moved an arm to catch the strange woman before she could run away. Under the jacket he felt a wet, sticky patch along her abdomen. Blood. His. That complicated matters. He couldn't very well send her back to the party like this.

"A problem?" the security guard asked.

"There's, ah, something different about the dress." Lev looked down at Esana.

Her smile could have ended wars. Or started them.

"There was a zipper there earlier this evening. Before our little reunion party."

"Ah." The security guard closed his notebook. "You've been very helpful," he said sarcastically.

"I'm so sorry, officer," Esana said, pulling away from Lev's touch. "Can I do more? I know this building very well. There's a third-story exit on the south side that connects to the restaurant next door. You can take the stairs there directly to the subway entrance. We use it all the time to get prominent guests in and out. I'll show you."

Lev pinched the fabric on her dress between his fingers, trying to keep her from running away.

She reached for the jacket as if she was going to forget the broken zipper and hurry to help.

"I know the entrance," Cecil said. He gave Esana a hurt look. "I'd be happy to show them."

"You're such a delight, Cecil."

The smile Esana gave him cured the man's melancholy. Poor fool thought he had a chance with her.

Lev found it very unpleasant. "Cecil, could you call us a car? I'm…"—he gave Esana the slow once over she'd treated him to—"…interested in going somewhere quieter."

Esana's surface thoughts found this perfectly agreeable, but there was no attraction there. No interest in him. Her pulse didn't leap at the chance to take advantage of him in any way. It was like she had a to-do list and somewhere at the bottom had found the words 'Save Lev' and decided to get it finished before she went home to wash her hair.

"My treasure, you don't mind going somewhere else tonight, do you?" he asked.

She stood on tiptoe so she was almost close enough to kiss. "How could I object?"

"I'll have the car ready in a moment," Cecil said quickly.

"I'll get the rest of the wine," Esana said. She nodded politely to the officers and slipped back into the darkness of the balcony.

"Cecil," Lev said, "I am leaving early so there will be no gossip. Do you understand?"

The man's eyes went wide with fright. "Naturally, Sevastionovich. No one will hear of this from me."

"Thank you, I appreciate discretion. This really was only a reunion."

Esana came back with the half-empty wine bottle and walked down the stairs with him, one hand pressing the jacket close around her.

She climbed into the car without a word and sat stoically beside him for the short drive back to his family's residence.

It was only when they were inside and the doors were closed that her sweet, lovestruck expression slipped away and the real Esana appeared.

She pulled off the jacket and hung it over the back of a chair. "Will that be all for the evening, Sevastionovich?"

"No." Lev sat on the edge of the table, not trusting himself to the comfort of a chair. "Tell me why you did this."

She raised an eyebrow. "It's my job to see the annual party runs smoothly. Finding the president's son passed out or dead from blood loss would be an unacceptable outcome for the evening.

Now you're home safe and my job is done."

"What about the security officers? Or the gunshot?"

"What about them?"

It was his turn to be surprised. There was nothing behind her words. Not a single flicker of emotion. "Don't you have questions?"

"Sevastionovich, I know your record. You were a traveling teacher and humanitarian since college. Do you know what's required for a teaching accreditation on this planet? An empath score of Skilled or higher.

"The highest national export for our solar system is empaths trained in espionage of one form or another. The most common cover for an espionage agent from this region is teacher. The most common plot line for a romance story for the past nineteen years has been a Returned Spy Finds Love. For nearly two decades this has dominated the national consciousness. Anyone with the ability to add two and two together knows what happened to you.

"You were an empath, you were offered a job, it worked out until they remembered you're a dirty foreigner, and now you're home where your family name can protect you."

"That is… an interesting view."

"And," she continued, "the bullet was poorly aimed but managed to take out whatever tracker you'd been tagged with, which is either very good luck or very good planning. Either way, you'll live through the night." There was no hint she cared if he lived or died.

"There's nothing you want to know?"

"I'm not paid to ask questions, Sevastionovich."

That name again. Sevastionovich. Son of Sevastion. Owned and belonging to Sevastion Aleksiev. "Lev," he said. "Call me Lev. And at least let me have your dress cleaned."

"I have a uterus. I know how to get blood out of clothes."

"So practical. Do you plan to go home like this?"

She glanced down at her clothes and there was a hint of consternation.

"Allow me to offer you something to change into, my treasure."

"I doubt you have anything in your closet my size, my heart." The look she gave him was sharp and biting. "Now, if you have no further need of me, Sevastionovich, I'll be going."

"Lev." He stood and moved to block the exit. "Stay. Change. We need to talk."

Her dark eyes studied him but gave nothing away.

It had been years since he'd met someone so collected and unreadable.

If he ever had. "You realize that if any of those men were empaths, they would have read your lie."

"What lie?" Esana radiated innocence. He could feel it, the complete and perfect belief that she had not lied. "I worked at the resort. Your family summered there. The guests flirted with the staff all the time. I'm certain that, at some point, you kissed a dark-haired girl surrounded by the smell of honeysuckle."

"True, but it wasn't you."

"Can you prove that?" Esana tilted her head and widened her eyes. It was a very calculated gesture, but it looked natural. If he couldn't feel her thinking about it, he would have been fooled.

He nodded. "How did you know the house color?"

"There's a picture of your family in front of it in your brother's office and I have an excellent memory."

"The girl I kissed?"

"Over eighty percent of the female wait staff at the resort had dark hair. The likelihood of a neighborhood busybody noticing you kissing one would be over seventy-two percent. If the security officers ask, they'll find a witness."

Lev took her hand. "So calculated. Come here. You can't go home like that. Someone will notice you leaving here covered in blood."

There was a mute resistance and then she followed along begrudgingly to his rooms. "I'm sure I can find a shirt you can wear. I'll have the dress laundered discreetly."

"I can handle it."

"Without anyone noticing the blood on the front?" Doubtful.

"I wasn't going to wear the dress again anyway."

He looked at her again. "That would be a shame, my charm."

Anger flared behind her blank eyes. "Feel free to drop the act, Sevastionovich."

"Lev," he insisted as he held out a white shirt. "You can change in the washroom."

"You're too kind, sir." She gave him a mocking bow and sashayed through his room.

The door clicked shut between them and he heard the soft whisper of cloth across skin. He kept his thoughts obscured. "You're not an empath, are you, Miss Esana?"

"No." Quick and cutting. "I'd have significantly better job options if I were gifted."

"And, your lover, how will you explain tonight to them?"

"There's no need to explain to anyone. I'm comfortably single." The door opened. "How will you explain to your girlfriend?"

He raised an eyebrow, mimicking her earlier expression. "I haven't had one in the better part of a year. So, like you, no explanation is necessary. You are certain you have no talents?"

"My mind is dead as a tree's," she said without emotion. "I have it on good authority that I'm an evolutionary failure. But everyone in my family is like this. Genetics." She shrugged.

"No mind is dead. Some are quieter than others, but I should be able to get some reading off you."

She stared deep into his eyes, letting the silence fill the room around them. "Why? I feel nothing, so there is nothing to read."

Lev smiled. That had been a lie. There'd been a tug to her words, a hint of emotion. She was hiding something from him very, very well. "You're an interesting person, my charm."

"Esana!"

"Lev."

Her eyes closed for a moment and the anger he should have felt wasn't there. "Sir, must you insist on being informal?"

He tilted his head to the side as he looked her up and down, long tan legs bare beneath his white shirt, a hint of white lace corsetry hidden behind his buttons, her dark hair tussled and wavy. "Under the circumstances, my light, I think formality would be rather coarse. This is not a business transaction."

"It's not a lover's exchange either."

"Perhaps a simple moment shared between friends, then."

"Where's my purse?" Esana muttered. She hurried back to the living room, moving faster than he could keep up.

By the time he turned the corner, she was knotting a scarf around her waist and rolling up the sleeves. She pirouetted for him. "Thoughts?"

He smiled, letting admiration run under his words. "You look divine, Esana. Stunningly beautiful."

"Hmm." Her eyes narrowed. "I was going for casual fun at the club."

"Only at a very nice club."

She lifted a shoulder in a shrug. "I have a stable job. I can afford the good clubs sometimes. Is there anything further, Se—" Her lips twisted at his look. "Sir?"

"You are certain you're loyal to no one?"

"Only to your father's company, sir."

"I don't need to write a thank you note to anyone?"

"No one at all, sir." She walked towards the door.

"I'll see you tomorrow?"

Her steps slowed only by a fraction. "If you're well enough for work, sir."

The door opened and his brother walked in, a woman hanging on his arm.

"Sevastionovich-ile!" Esana stepped back quickly.

"Esana?" His brother looked her up and down. "I thought you were still at the concert."

"Oh, I, ah, spilled some wine on my gown." She held up the folded mess. "I was going to go home, but your brother saw me and offered me a chance to change. Here."

That was a terrible lie and they both knew it. Thankfully his brother was more than a little drunk. Issyk waved a hand. "Stay! Stay, Esana and meet…" He peered at the woman on his arm.

"Bettani." She giggled, her thoughts bouncing higher than the clouds on whatever cocktail of drugs and liquor his brother had provided.

"Bettani!" Issyk shouted. "We will have a party here! Just us lovers."

Esana was already shaking her head. "It's not like that, Sevastionovich-ile. Your brother and I are not—"

Issyk grabbed her by the arm and pushed her towards Lev. "Stay. Make my brother smile."

Anger touched Esana's thoughts.

"Give me a moment," Lev murmured in her ear. "Can you take Bettani home?"

"Yes." Esana's words were tight with frustration.

He ran a hand along her shoulder, trying to whisper calming thoughts to her mind.

The response was a stinging retort that shocked him.

Mind dead?

Not even close.

THE MAKING OF
HERE SHE LIES

This is going to date me and the story but here it goes…

Have you ever watched a Turkish dizi (drama)? I hadn't until one day a Tumblr mutual started posting an obsessive amount of GIFs. I was invested in the story before I even had a clue what the title was or where in the world it was from. Body language breaks all barriers.

As it turned out, the dizi was the very popular *Erkenci Kuş,* starring Can Yamen and Demet Özdemir, which starts with Demet's character, Sanem, going to a company party and being kissed by a stranger in the dark.

Yeah… There's a lot of issues with consent there. But I still loved the idea.

I played with it, trying to take the parts I loved and turn them into something a little more sci-fi and consensual. In the end I had an opening and not much else. With a little polish it made a cute short story—a moment of promise, and nothing more.

Read more by Liana Brooks!

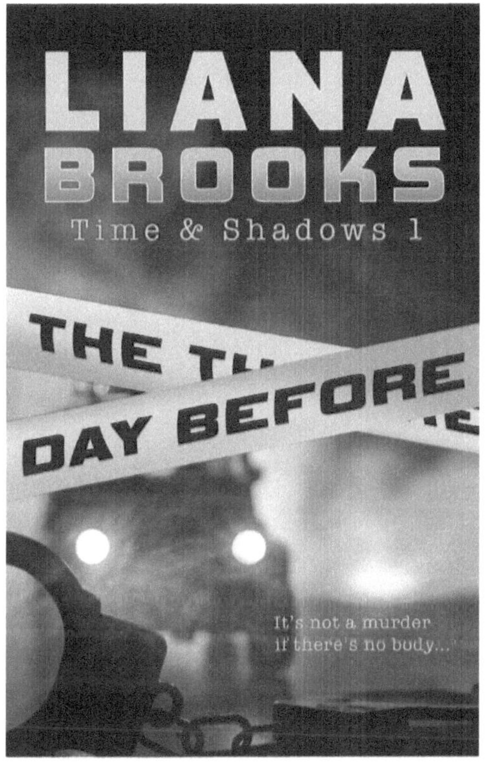

THE DAY BEFORE
CHAPTER 1

The late Dr. Everett's Many-World inter-pretation of quantum mechanics is notable for two reasons. One, it is laughably simple. Two, it is almost correct. Had Dr. Everett recalled that there is no particle without a wave, our research would now be an exercise in tedium. Alas, it is the failing of generations past that they did not consider the wave form and thus anticipate the eventual collapse of iterations not held stable by Pointer States, or ein-selection nodes.

~ Excerpt from Lectures on the Movement of Time *by Dr. Abdul Emir I1–20740413*

Friday May 17, 2069 / Alabama District 3 / Commonwealth of North America

With an asthmatic wheeze, the engine died. It figured. Stuck in a man's craw, it did. This truck had been his daddy's and his pappy's, and before the Commonwealth government forced him to replace the diesel engine with the newfangled water doo-hickey, he was certain he'd pass the truck on to his son.

He'd been playing under the hood of trucks since he was six, and now he was stranded. Embarrassing, that's what it was. He climbed out of the cab to check the engine out of habit. The ice-blue block of modern fuel efficiency stared back. Three hundred bucks it'd cost him, straight from his pocket.

Oh, there was a government subsidy, all right. A priority list. Major population centers, they said. Unite the countries of the Commonwealth on a timeline, they said. And what did all that mean?

It meant the damn Yankees got upgraded cities and free cars before the ink was dry on the Constitution, and what about the little man? Nobody thought about the working class. No one cared about a man covered in oil and grease anymore.

He thumbed his cell phone on.

No reception. Figured.

So much for the era of new prosperity.

He'd hoof it. There was a little town about five miles down the road where he could call Ricky to bring a tow truck. It would have been cheaper to pay the diesel fines than get all this fixed.

Off schedule. Over budget. Son of a—

He stared at the distant oaks. Well, it wasn't going to get any cooler.

He grabbed his wallet and keys from the cab of his truck. The tree line looked like a good spot to answer a call from nature, then he'd see if there was a shortcut through to town.

A meadowlark sang. Not a bad day for a hike. Would've been better if it weren't so dammed hot, but at least the humidity was low. He wouldn't like to walk in a summer monsoon, not at his age, with arthritis playing up.

Under a sprawling pine tree, he unzipped his pants. As an afterthought, he glanced down to make sure he wouldn't stir up a hill of fire ants.

A hand lay next to his boots.

He blinked, zipped his pants slowly, and turned around. "Hello?"

Cicadas chirped in answer.

"Are you drunk?"

The quiet field that had looked so peaceful only moments before was now eerily sinister. He nudged the hand with his foot. It was swollen and pale and crusted with blood, just like a prop out of a horror movie.

Maybe it was a good idea to *run* to the next town.

· · · · · · · · · · · · · · · ● ● ● ● ● ● · · · · · · · · · · ·

They say a coward dies a thousand deaths, a brave man only one. Where underpaid, overstressed probationary agents fell in that spectrum, Sam wasn't sure, but she'd bet her last dollar she was headed down the slippery slope of a thousand cowardly deaths. Any sensible person would not have picked up their work phone after eight on a Friday night, or at least would have the spine to tell their boss they weren't going to work on the weekend.

Which was exactly what Senior Agent Marrins wanted Sam to do.

On a curving old road between two towns untouched by a century of change, in a place where streetlights were still considered new technology, some broke-down trucker had found a body. Three miles west, and it would have been someone else's problem. In any other district, it would have been the senior agent's problem, and she would have tagged along to get the work experience needed for promotion.

Sam didn't work in any other district, though. She worked in Senior Agent Marrins'. Which was why she was driving out to this rural stretch of road.

The wash of the Milky Way glittering overhead was beautiful, if you were into that sort of thing. Sam would have preferred the gaudy show of lights in any major city in any major first-world country. "Saint Jude, pray for me who am so miserable," she whispered as the crime scene came into view. Three police cars, an eighteen-wheeler, and an ambulance... Not your typical Friday night in Alabama District 3.

An unfamiliar police officer knocked on the window and made a circular motion. "Ma'am, this is a crime scene. I'm going to ask you to keep moving."

"Officer, I'm Agent Samantha Rose from the Commonwealth Bureau of Investigation, and I'm going to ask you who the hell you think would drive out this far from civilization at this time of night."

He blinked at her.

"Precisely. Would you please step away from my car and call the officer in charge? Thanks." Men. They weren't all idiots, but she'd seen little evidence that these illiterate hicks could prove it.

"Rose?"

Sam closed her car door and looked around. "Detective Altin?" A man who towered a full foot over her should not have been able to hide.

"Behind you."

She spun and almost tripped into the older man. "I thought you were going to the movies with your wife."

"She took the kids instead. Twenty-five years married to the force, she'll forgive me." Altin's teeth flashed as he grinned. "You just won me a bet. The sergeant from Cherokee County was certain Marrins would come out himself."

"Has the sergeant *met* Agent Marrins?" Sam asked. "The only time that man hustles is when there's a fresh box of donuts at the secretary's desk." She shrugged. "I live on this side of the district. Marrins wrote this off as effective delegation of resources."

"I thought Marrins would at least try to get this on his resume. The last time we had a homicide where there were actual questions was that horror-house case that hit all the national news stations, and that was over a decade ago. Isn't that how the bureau promotes?" Altin's grin widened.

Sam rolled her eyes. "Yeah, but a dumped clone isn't a homicide investigation. It's littering."

"Who said it was a clone?"

"Agent Marrins."

"He's psychic now?" The detective raised a skeptical eyebrow.

"He said the police called him about a dumped clone, and I needed to sort it out."

Altin shook his head. "I wouldn't jump to conclusions. People might be eager to dump their clones before the Caye Law goes into effect and they have to pay a tax on them. But there are organ-donation stations that take the clones for free. No one's going to drive all the way out here to chop up a clone and dump it. Too much work."

"There are still reasons why someone

might skip the legal methods of disposal." Like having an illegal clone. Her first case fresh out of the academy in Langley had been busting an illegal-clone ring using stolen DNA to sell fetish slaves to stalkers. Rows of growth-accelerated children who went from infant to adolescent in under a week, half-starved and chained to the walls of the California mansion's attic.

Their vacant stares still haunted her dreams.

She crossed herself out of habit, then pulled on her forensic gloves. "Okay—let's go meet Jane Doe."

Keep reading! Head to
www.inkprintpress.com/
lianabrooks/timeshadows/
daybefore/
to buy your copy now!

ABOUT THE AUTHOR

LIANA BROOKS is definitely not a spy. Ignore the lockpick on her desk, that's just for decoration…

By day, Liana enjoys writing science fiction in every form, from sprawling space operas romances (the *Fleet of Malik* series) to the antics of a super-powered family (the *Heroes and Villains* series).

Liana also maintains a soft spot for paranormal romances. She writes the popular *All I Want For Christmas* novellas, including *All I Want For Christmas Is A Werewolf* and *All I Want For Christmas Is A Reaper*.

You can learn more about her and her books at www.LianaBrooks.com.

INKLETS

Collect them all! Released on the 1st and 15th of each month.

Shadows
NEVER LIE
AMY LAURENS

Here She Lies
LIANA BROOKS

Perfect
Destruction
An Age Of Unicorns Story
AMY LAURENS

What Blood
Can Do
AMY LAURENS

Dancer, Dreamer
Seer
LIANA BROOKS

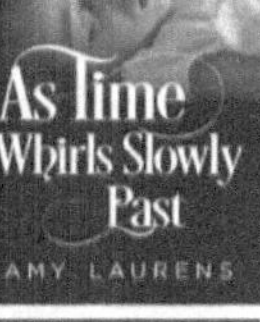
As Time
Whirls Slowly
Past
AMY LAURENS

Far More
Satisfying
Than Hell
AMY LAURENS

Just
Another Day
In Hell
LIANA BROOKS

Moon AND
Morning
AMY LAURENS

INKLET #088
Some
Impropriety
Expected
AMY LAURENS

INKLET #089
NEON SNOW
LIANA BROOKS

INKLET #090
Reincarnation
LIANA BROOKS

INKLET #091
More Than
Mushrooms
AMY LAURENS

DOUBLE ISSUE
INKLET #092
How To Make A Star
& The World Ended
LIANA BROOKS

INKLET #093
CAUGHT
IN THE ACT
AMY LAURENS

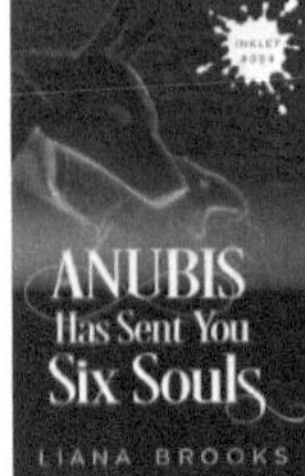

INKLET #094
ANUBIS
Has Sent You
Six Souls
LIANA BROOKS

INKLET #095
PRAYER TO A
GODDESS
LIANA BROOKS

INKLET #096
Love In The
Time Of Corona
AMY LAURENS

www.ingramcontent.com/pod-product-compliance
Lightning Source LLC
Chambersburg PA
CBHW030811190726
48285CB00003B/1132